CHAMP AND MAJOR:

First Dogs

BY JOY MCCULLOUGH   ILLUSTRATED BY SHEYDA ABVABI BEST

DIAL BOOKS FOR YOUNG READERS

Champ waits patiently while his dad works.

For Owen and Athena and every good dog (which is all of them)—J.M.

For Jeff—S.A.B.

Dial Books for Young Readers
An imprint of Penguin Random House LLC, New York

First published in the United States of America by Dial Books for Young Readers,
an imprint of Penguin Random House LLC, 2021

Visit us online at penguinrandomhouse.com.

Library of Congress Cataloging-in-Publication Data is available.

Printed in the United States of America

ISBN 9780593407141

10 9 8 7 6 5 4 3 2 1

Design by Jennifer Kelly
Text set in Alegreya and Fink

The illustrations for this book were created digitally with the help of lots of iced coffee.

Champ's dad has a really important job.
And so does Champ. Champ's job is to make sure
his dad doesn't work all the time!

It's a really big job for one dog.

But when work is over, it's time to play!

Major isn't much help at first.

After a while, a new dog comes to help.

But Champ can show him the ropes.

More about shelter pets

The Bidens adopted Major from the Delaware Humane Association. There are similar organizations all around the world. Sometimes they're called humane societies, animal shelters, or rescue organizations. All of them offer the opportunity to adopt pets that need homes, instead of buying from a breeder or a pet store.

Here are some reasons it's a great idea to adopt:

- **Save a life:** Around 3.3 million dogs and 3.2 million cats enter animal shelters every year. Sadly, around 1.5 million of them are put to sleep because there is no room in the shelters. Every time an animal is adopted, there's space for another in the shelter!

- **Get a dog that's already trained:** Major was a puppy when he went home with the Bidens, so he still needed training. But at a shelter, you can get a dog who's a little bit older and already trained. Or a lot older—senior dogs have extra experience giving love and snuggles!

- **Make sure you're a good fit:** Many shelters offer the option to foster a dog first, as the Bidens did with Major. Then, if the dog turns out to be a good match for your family, you can adopt. If not, the shelter can find a new home for the dog!

TE HOUSE WITH PETS. HERE ARE SOME STANDOUTS!

WILLIAM McKINLEY	THEODORE ROOSEVELT	WILLIAM HOWARD TAFT	WOODROW WILSON	FRANKLIN DELANO ROOSEVELT	GEORGE W. BUSH	BARACK OBAMA
1897–1901	1901–1909	1909–1913	1913–1921	1933–1945	2001–2009	2009–2017
President McKinley's parrot, Washington Post, could whistle the patriotic song "Yankee Doodle."	Teddy Roosevelt had a ton of pets: Horses, two cats, five guinea pigs, ten dogs, a pony, a lizard, a hen, a rat, a badger, a macaw, a pig, a black bear, a rabbit, a hyena, a barn owl, a one-legged rooster, snakes, and a flying squirrel!	President Taft had a cow named Pauline Wayne, whose milk was sold in tiny souvenir bottles so anyone could have a taste of the same milk as the president.	President Wilson kept a flock of 48 sheep that trimmed the White House lawn. Their wool was sold to benefit the Red Cross.	One of FDR's seven dogs was a German shepherd named Major, just like President Biden's Major!	George W. Bush's father, George H. W. Bush, was president before him. His dog Spotty's mother was Millie, the previous Bush's White House dog.	Barack Obama's Portuguese water dogs, Sunny and Bo, played with Champ at the White House.

Author's Note

When Joe Biden was campaigning to become Barack Obama's vice president, he promised his wife, Dr. Jill Biden, that if they won, they would adopt a puppy. The Obama-Biden ticket won, and in 2008, the Bidens adopted a German shepherd puppy they named Champ.

Champ lived with them in the vice president's residence, on the grounds of the United States Naval Observatory. He also got to visit the White House, where he played with President Obama's Portuguese water dogs, Sunny and Bo.

Ten years later, the Bidens' daughter, Ashley, saw that the Delaware Humane Association had received a litter of German shepherd puppies with some health problems and were looking for foster families. The Bidens called the shelter right away. Major joined the family in March of 2018 as a foster dog, and was adopted by November.

In November 2020, Champ and Major's dad, Joe Biden, was elected as the 46th President of the United States. Major would be the first shelter dog to ever live in the White House!

In January 2021, Champ and Major moved into the White House as First Dogs, joining a long line of presidential pets that have done the very important job of bringing fun, play, and rest to the White House.

ALL BUT TWO UNITED STATES PRESIDENTS SHARED

GEORGE WASHINGTON
1789–1797

The White House wasn't built yet when George Washington was president, but he had dogs, donkeys, horses, and a parrot at his home in Mount Vernon.

THOMAS JEFFERSON
1801–1809

Two grizzly bear cubs were gifted to President Jefferson and stayed at the White House for two months.

JOHN QUINCY ADAMS
1825–1829

First Lady Louisa Adams raised silkworms and spun silk from their thread!

MARTIN VAN BUREN
1837–1841

President Van Buren received two tiger cubs as a gift from the Sultan of Oman. He wanted to keep them at the White House, but Congress forced him to send them to the zoo.

JAMES BUCHANAN
1857–1861

President Buchanan was gifted a pair of bald eagles, the symbol of the United States. They did not stay at the White House for long, but lived out their lives at his home in Pennsylvania.

ABRAHAM LINCOLN
1861–1865

Jack the turkey was meant for a White House dinner, but Lincoln's son Tad convinced his father to spare the turkey's life and kept him as a pet.

ANDREW JOHNSON
1865–1869

No official pets, but befriended and fed some White House mice.

BENJAMIN HARRISON
1889–1893

President Harrison's House included goats, the collie, two opossums named Mr. Reciprocity, Mr. Protection, and two alligators.

And this time, they're home.

Champ can't wait to show Major around.

Everyone there does important work, but they
always have time to say hello!

Champ has visited the White House before,
when his dad was vice president.

And just in time, because their family's job is
about to get even more important!

With Champ's help, soon Major is ready.

Major doesn't need lessons on how to be a good friend.

Champ teaches Major everything he knows.